TRANSFORMERS PRIME

D1318365

SUPER SEARCH

Picture Puzzles, Mazes, and more

Reader's Digest
Children's Books®

New York, New York • Montréal, Québec • Bath, United Kingdom

AMAGING MAZES

Optimus Prime, the Autobots' leader, must reach his loyal soldier, Bumblebee before the Decepticons can launch an attack. Help Optimus by finding the path through the maze that takes you from START to END. You can only exit a space through the black triangle in each space. The legend on the left shows you which direction each triangle sends you next. You must go through the space with the Decepticon mask before you get to the END.

START

END

Bumblebee, Ratchet and Optimus must change from robot to vehicle mode in a hurry. Help them by using your finger to trace the lines from each robot to the correct vehicle.

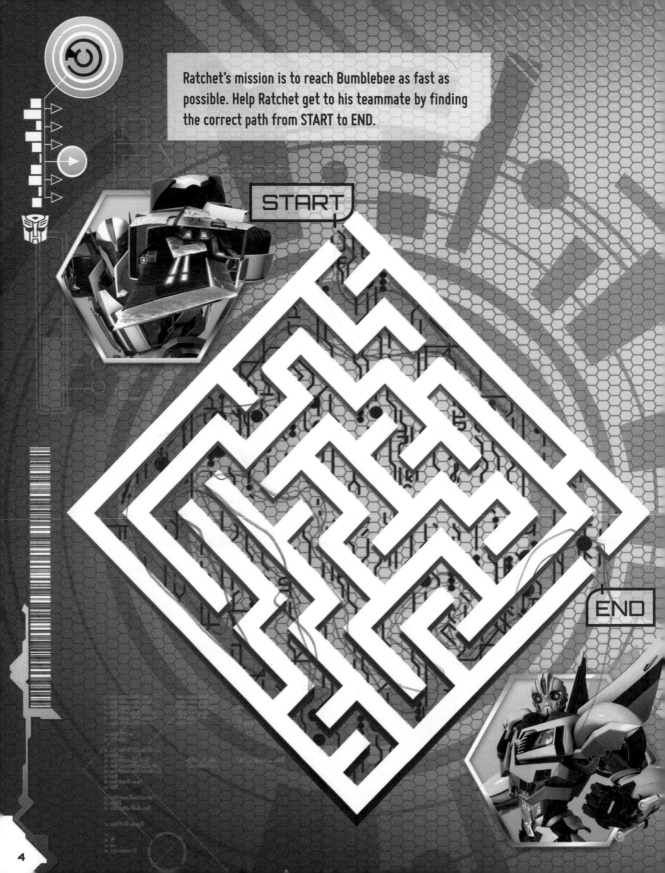

Ratchet's mission is to reach Bumblebee as fast as possible. Help Ratchet get to his teammate by finding the correct path from START to END.

START

END

The Decepticons' master spy, Soundwave, is on a top-secret mission to learn all he can about the Autobots' defenses. Help the Autobots by guiding Arcee through the maze from START to the END, so the brave Autobot can stop Soundwave before he gets away.

START

END

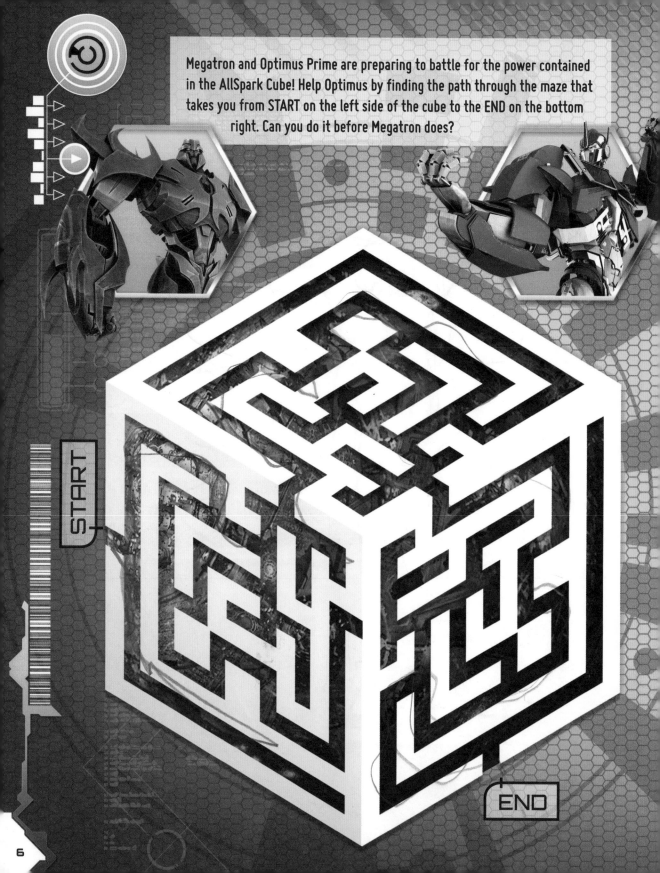

Megatron and Optimus Prime are preparing to battle for the power contained in the AllSpark Cube! Help Optimus by finding the path through the maze that takes you from START on the left side of the cube to the END on the bottom right. Can you do it before Megatron does?

START

END

Your mission: Find your way through the maze and avoid the Decepticons. Do that by following a path from START to END that is made up of only Autobot masks. You can move up, down, across, or diagonally.

START

END

Arcee and Bumblebee have been directed by Optimus to meet and team up for a mission against the Decepticons. Help Arcee get to her teammate by finding the path that goes from START to the END where Bumblebee waits.

END

START

Decepticon Alert! Starscream, Megatron, and Soundwave are about to change into vehicle mode. Can you identify each Decepticon's vehicle mode? Use your finger to trace the path from robot to vehicle.

Two Autobots teams—Optimus and Bumblebee, and Bulkhead and Arcee—are racing to the center of Cybertron, home planet of the Transformers. Can you lead each team to the Autobots mask in the middle of the maze. Use your finger to trace the right paths that lead each team from START the center of the maze.

START

START

The Decepticons have implanted a crippling virus into a circuit board in the Autobots' computer system, and you've got to help them find and disable it. Do that by finding the path from START to the virus, represented by the Decepticon mask. Then make your way back out of the maze to the END.

START

END

Sparks fly whenever Arcee and Starscream are locked in battle. These two battle scenes may look alike, but there are actually seven things that are different. Can you find them?

Whether in robot mode or in his guise as an alien jet fighter plane, Megatron always poses a dangerous challenge for any Autobot he encounters. Are you ready for a Megatron-sized challenge? Find seven things that are different in these two scenes.

Knock Out has just discovered that the Decepticons' Data Cylinders are empty.
Can you discover seven things that are different in these two pictures?

Optimus Prime is the biggest, strongest, and smartest of all the Transformers. When he's in his big-rig vehicle mode, he's a powerful sight to see. See if you can find seven differences between these two pictures.

Agent Fowler and Optimus Prime are determined to track down the Decepticons. Can you track down the seven things that are different in these two pictures?

In vehicle mode, Ratchet is an emergency medical vehicle. In robot mode, he's a powerful warrior in the fight against the Decepticons. Can you spot seven things that are different in these two pictures of Ratchet?

Along with Bulkhead, Wheeljack was once part of an awesome Autobots team of Wreckers. He's also the slightly mad scientist of the Autobots army. Can you spot seven things that are different in these two portraits of Wheeljack?

You can always count on some fireworks when Decepticon leader Megatron shows up, whether in alien fighter form or robot mode. Can you identify seven things that are different in these two close-ups of the Autobots' most fearsome foe?

As cunning and deadly as a poisonous spider, Airachnid is a villainess capable of dealing a stinging blow to a foe. If you dare, stare at these two pictures of this Decepticon and find seven things that are different

Ratchet may be the chief medical officer for the Autobots, but he's capable of causing major damage to Decepticons and their allies. Here are two pictures of Ratchet smashing a Vehicon who dared to take him on. Can you find the seven things that are different?

The Autobots—Optimus, Bumblebee, Bulkhead and Arcee—and Decepticon leader Megatron have slipped into the shadows as they prepare for battle. Can you match the robots on the left-hand page to the correct silhouette on the right-hand page?

Another battle is brewing between the Autobots and Decepticons in deep darkness so only their silhouettes are visible. Can you match the silhouettes with the correct robots?

QUADRANT QUIZ

Below you will find four squares or quadrants that are part of the big picture of Optimus Prime. Can you identify where each quadrant or square appears in the picture of Optimus on the right?

Ratchet's on high alert for Decepticons. Can you identify where the four quadrants below are located in the big picture of Ratchet on the left?

Knock Out, once Starscream's second-in-command, is one of the few Decepticons who changes into a car in vehicle mode. Can you find where the four quadrants below fit into the big picture of Knockout on the right?

Who is the most evil—and deadly—of all the Transformers? Megatron, of course. See if you can identify where the four quadrants below are located in the large picture of Megatron in full fighting mode on the left.

When Megatron unleashes a blast from his arsenal of weapons, especially his Fusion Cannon, better get out of the way! But before you do, see if you can locate the four quadrants below in the big picture of the Decepticon leader on the right.

Nemesis, the Decepticons' giant, weapon-laden spaceship, also serves as their base. Before it speeds away, see if you can locate the four quadrants below in the big picture on the left.

Q+A

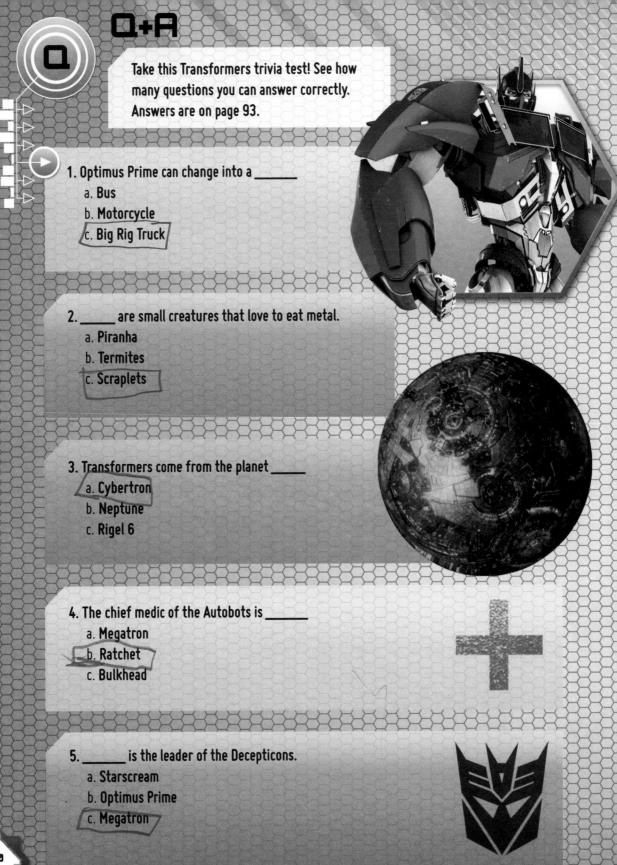

Take this Transformers trivia test! See how many questions you can answer correctly. Answers are on page 93.

1. Optimus Prime can change into a _____
   a. Bus
   b. Motorcycle
   c. Big Rig Truck

2. _____ are small creatures that love to eat metal.
   a. Piranha
   b. Termites
   c. Scraplets

3. Transformers come from the planet _____
   a. Cybertron
   b. Neptune
   c. Rigel 6

4. The chief medic of the Autobots is _____
   a. Megatron
   b. Ratchet
   c. Bulkhead

5. _____ is the leader of the Decepticons.
   a. Starscream
   b. Optimus Prime
   c. Megatron

6. All Transformers need _____ for power.
    a. Water
    b. Energon
    c. Spinach

7. Miko is an exchange student from _____
    a. China
    b. England
    c. Japan

8 .The Decepticon Starscream changes into a _____
    a. Helicopter
    b. Blimp
    c. Fighter Jet

9. The name of the Autobots' secret base is _____
    a. The Pit
    b. Autobot Outpost Omega One
    c. The Garage

10. The only human who can understand Bumblebee's speech is _____
    a. Jack
    b. Raf
    c. Agent Fowler

11. Jack works at a fast food restaurant called _____
    a. Prince of Burgers
    b. Maccadam's Old Oil House
    c. K.O. Burger

12. Whenever someone breaks one of his tools,
Ratchet says, _____
    a. "Autobots, roll out!"
    b. "I needed that!"
    c. "Peace through tyranny!"

13. When in her robot form, Airachnid looks
like a giant _____
    a. Wasp
    b. Shark
    c. Spider

14. In her free time, Miko likes to _____
    a. Play electric guitar
    b. Knit
    c. Collect stamps

15. The Decepticons' master spy is _____
    a. Bumblebee
    b. Soundwave
    c. Knock Out

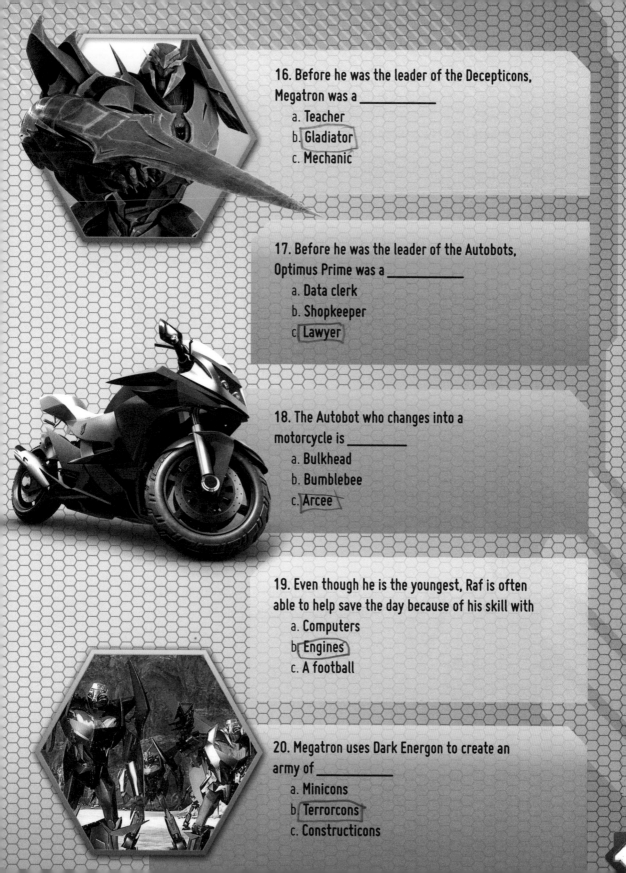

16. Before he was the leader of the Decepticons, Megatron was a _____
   a. Teacher
   b. Gladiator
   c. Mechanic

17. Before he was the leader of the Autobots, Optimus Prime was a _____
   a. Data clerk
   b. Shopkeeper
   c. Lawyer

18. The Autobot who changes into a motorcycle is _____
   a. Bulkhead
   b. Bumblebee
   c. Arcee

19. Even though he is the youngest, Raf is often able to help save the day because of his skill with
   a. Computers
   b. Engines
   c. A football

20. Megatron uses Dark Energon to create an army of _____
   a. Minicons
   b. Terrorcons
   c. Constructicons

21. The Decepticon base is a giant spaceship called _____
   a. The Nemesis
   b. Trypticon
   c. The Ark

22. Laserbeak is one of the Decepticon Deployers controlled by _____
   a. Starscream
   b. Soundwave
   c. Breakdown

23. The youngest Autobot on Team PRIME is _____
   a. Ratchet
   b. Bumblebee
   c. Optimus Prime

24. Long ago on Cybertron, Megatron was good friends with _____
   a. Starscream
   b. Soundwave
   c. Optimus Prime

25. The next time you see a yellow and black muscle car on the road, it might just be _____
   a. Megatron
   b. Bumblebee
   c. Bulkhead

26. One of the strongest, and clumsiest, Autobots is _____
    a. Optimus Prime
    b. Arcee
    c. Bulkhead

27. The Decepticon medic who hates getting his paint
scratched is _____
    a. Breakdown
    b. Knock Out
    c. Airachnid

28. Arcee and Jack are often chased by Decepticon
troopers called _____
    a. Vehicons
    b. Team Prime
    c. Combaticons

29. The Autobots can transport themselves anywhere on
Earth using the _____
    a. GroundBridge
    b. Transporter
    c. Titanic

30. Optimus Prime carries in his chest an ancient artifact
and source of wisdom, called _____
    a. The AllSpark
    b. The Matrix of Leadership
    c. The Requiem Blaster

GRID MASTER

Bulkhead may be a gentle giant when it comes to human friends like Miko. But Bulkhead is a fierce fighting machine packed with plenty of muscle power. Can you figure out where the nine squares below are located in the large picture of Bulkhead on the right?

Starscream is dangerous and sneaky, which makes him a constant threat to the Autobots. He's also Decepticon leader Megatron's right-hand robot. Can you identify where each of the nine squares below are located in the picture of Starscream on the left?

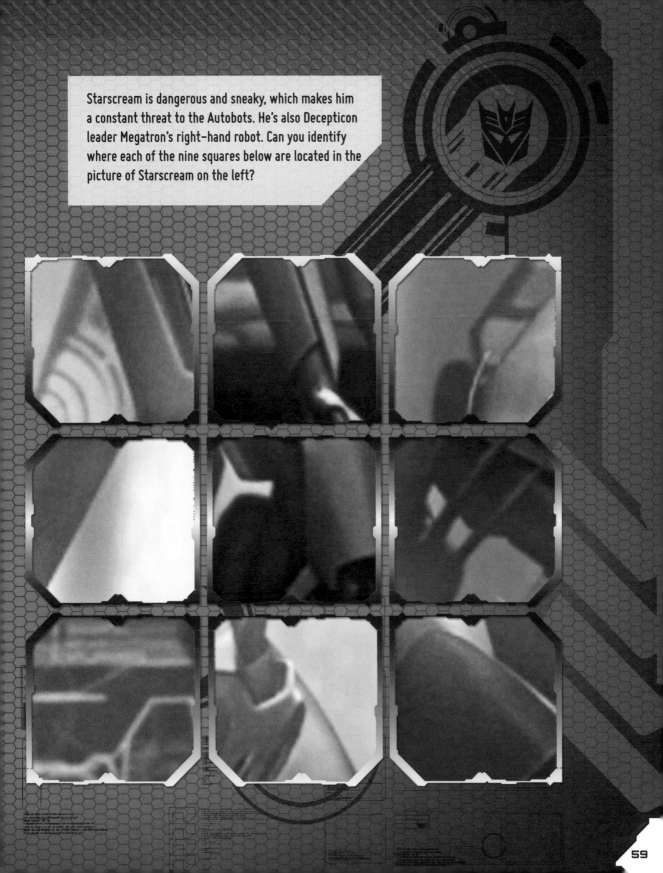

Sleek, fast, and powerful, Arcee is Optimus Prime's trusted go-to girl, and one awesome motorcycle in vehicle mode. Can you locate the nine squares below in the big picture of Arcee on the left?

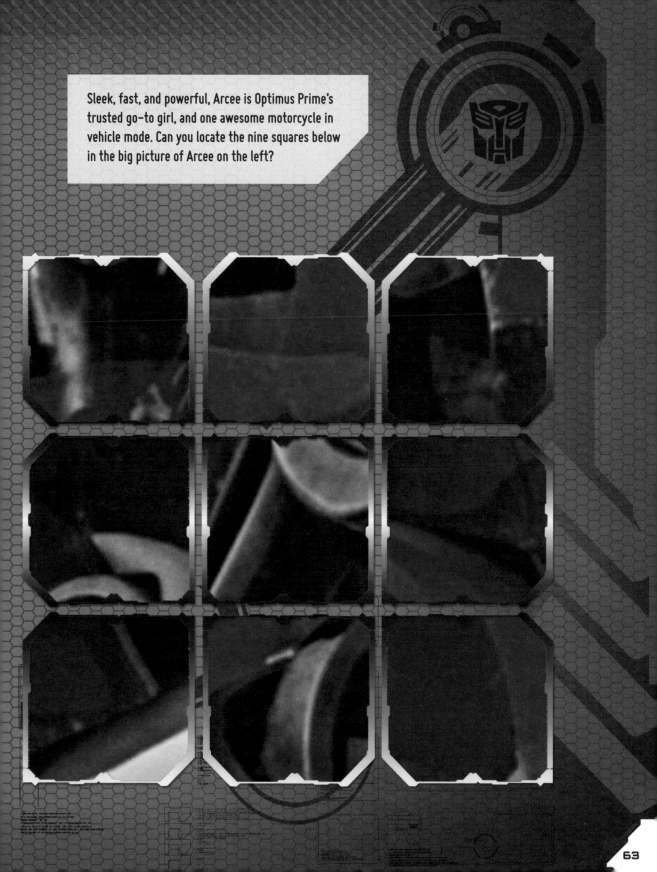

Terrorcons are zombie-like robot soldiers under the influence of Dark Energon. Examine the nine squares below and see if you can locate them in the picture of the two Terrorcons on the right.

FIND THE IMPOSTER

Imposters have infiltrated the ranks of the Autobots and Decepticons. On the next seven pages you will see pictures of various robots. Find the imposter on each page by finding the one picture that differs from the other three.

MEMORY CHALLENGE

Test yourself in this Transformers memory challenge. Lift the flaps two at a time and see what's underneath. If you find a matching pair, leave the flaps up. If they're not a match close the flaps. Then keep lifing the flaps two at a time to find all the matching pairs of symbols.

MEMORY CHALLENGE 2

Now that you've warmed up on the first Memory Challenge, see how long it takes you to find all the matching symbols in this challenge.

MEMORY CHALLENGE 3

Now that you've successfully completed the first two Memory Challenges, you're ready to take it to the next level. See if you can find the all the matching pairs of symbols in this challenge.

MEMORY CHALLENGE 4

Are you ready for the final challenge? Now that you are a practiced pro, see how fast you can find the matching pairs of symbols in this last challenge.

MIX AND MATCH

On each of the following six pages you will see a mixed up Transformers picture. It features the top half of one robot with the bottom half of a completely different one. Using colors and other features, see if you can guess the two Transformers in each mixed up picture.

2-3

4-5

6-7

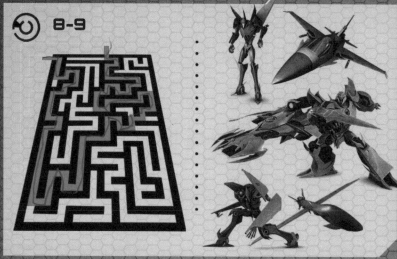

10-11

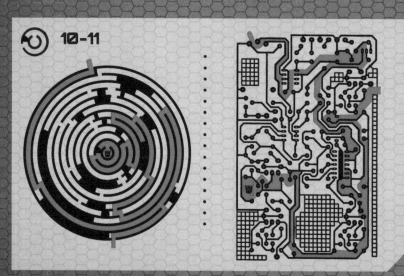

48-49

50-55

1. c	2. c	3. b	4. a	5. c	6. b
7. c	8. c	9. b	10. b	11. c	12. b
13. a	14. c	15. b	16. b	17. a	18. c
19. a	20. b	21. a	22. b	23. b	24. c
25. b	26. a	27. c	28. b	29. a	30. b

56-57

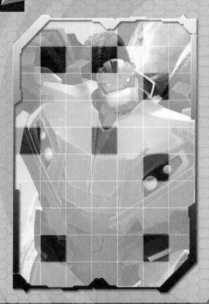

58-59

60-61

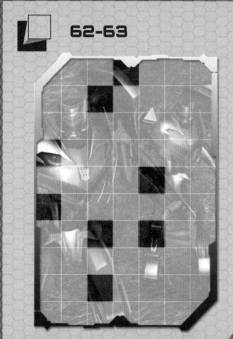

62-63

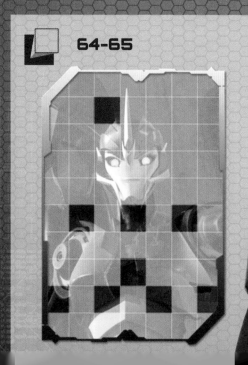

64-65

❖ 66

❖ 67

❖ 68

❖ 69

❖ 70

❖ 71

❖ 72

⤭ 81

Bumblebee

Arcee

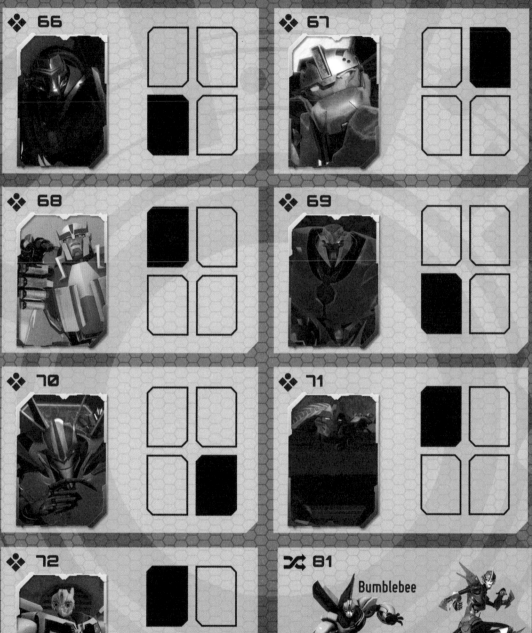

82

Optimus Prime

Bumblebee

83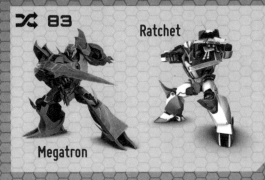

Ratchet

Megatron

84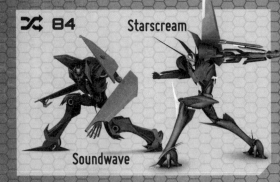

Starscream

Soundwave

85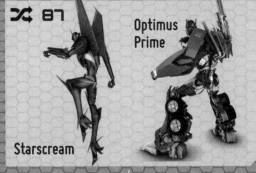

Bulkhead

Ratchet

86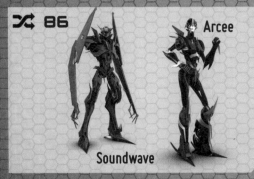

Arcee

Soundwave

87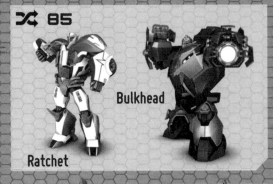

Optimus Prime

Starscream

88

Bulkhead

Megatron